BLODEUWEDD

by

Ogmore Batt

The woodcut engravings reproduced in this text are taken from Cirker, B. (ed.): *1800 Woodcuts by Thomas Bewick and his school (1990)*, published by Dover Publications, Inc., New York.

The photograph of Llech Ronw on page 48 was taken by the author balanced rather precariously on a stony bank of the babbling Afon Bryn Saeth in 1994 in Ardudwy.

The pen & ink illustration on page 14 of the flowers of Oak and the flowers of Meadowsweet and the flowers of Broom is taken from Michael Senior: *Gods and Heroes in North Wales: A Mythological Guide (1993)*, published by Gwasg Carreg Gwalch, Llanrwst, Gwynedd, and is used by kind permission of Myrddin ap Dafydd.

The author gratefully acknowledges the financial support of the North West Wales Employment Zone Partnership, Parc Menai, Bangor, for its contribution to the production costs of this book. Without such generous funding, this First Impression just would not have been possible.

ISBN: 0 86243 587 0

Dinas is an imprint of Y Lolfa

y|**Lol**fa

Published and printed in Wales
by Y Lolfa Cyf., Talybont, Ceredigion SY24 5AP
e-mail ylolfa@ylolfa.com
website www.ylolfa.com
tel. (01970) 832 304
fax 832 782
isdn 832 813

BLODEUWEDD

by

Ogmore Batt

A novel re-telling of the legendary Welsh tale

*– Metempsychosis, he said, frowning. It's Greek. From the Greeks.
It means the transmigration of souls.*
– O, rocks! she said. Tell us in plain words.

Bloom attempts to explain the world to Molly
in bed at breakfast at 7 Eccles Street, Dublin,
on Thursday June 16th 1904, in James Joyce's
Ulysses (1922)

To Beth

CONTENTS

Introduction: Mimicking *The Mabinogion*

BLODEUWEDD

INTRODUCTION: Mimicking *The Mabinogion*

The '**Mabinogion**'! Does the reader not know it? There's *ignorance* for you! Well then, I'd better explain it.

'The Mabinogion' is the title in everyday use for a collection of eleven Welsh tales, written down some time between 1050 and 1170, and this anonymous medieval manuscript has long been recognised as a masterpiece of European prose literature. It was written, in Welsh, when Europe was largely illiterate. It is difficult to exaggerate the literary gift of the monks who first inked the first draft and gave it its impact. The word 'Mabinogion', itself, however, is modern. It was bestowed upon the collection, very felicitously, by mistake, by Lady Charlotte Guest of Dowlais, as the over-arching title for her celebrated English translations which appeared in three volumes between 1838 and 1849. But the name 'Mabinogion' she gave was a misnomer! Charlotte misnamed it! It is not the plural, as she thought it was, of the Welsh word *Mabinogi* which *is* the word that describes the four inter-linked stories in the Welsh anthology, The Four Branches (as they are called in *Cymraeg*) of the Mabinogi (you see). 'Mabinogi' derives from the Welsh word *mab* meaning youth and *Mabinogi* meant, first, 'A Tale of Youth', then later 'A Tale of A Hero', and, finally, just 'Tale', or, simply, a 'Story'. A 'Branch' of The Mabinogi can be interpreted as designating or signalling the start of a 'Part of The Story'. *Pedair Cainc y Mabinogi* (The Four Branches of The Mabinogi) are, in order of their appearance, the stories of:

> *Pwyll, Prince of Dyfed;*
> *Branwen, daughter of Llŷr;*
> *Manawydan, son of Llŷr;*
> *Math, son of Mathonwy.*

These manuscript stories are the written-down re-workings of old orally-told stories told by peripatetic storytellers who travelled in Wales and they (the writings) represent the only extant remnant of what was, earlier, no doubt, A Bloody Great Epic ('The Full Story') allegedly all about King Pryderi, son of Pwyll, Prince of Dyfed, King of South Wales. *Pedair Cainc y Mabinogi* is what survived. The Welsh *Epic*, however, in its entirety, the epic is lost. All we have is *The Mabinogion*.

Blodeuwedd is a novel re-telling, in the contemporary vernacular, of the astonishing second part of The Fourth Branch of The Mabinogi (The *Math ap Mathonwy* Story). This was clearly once a separate story (a branch, a chapter) in its own right. The story begins very dramatically with an incestuous begetting, King Math's test of virginity, and immediately that's done, Arianrhod gives birth and Gwydion the Magician incubates the after-birth. *Blodeuwedd* tells the fateful and sometimes quite tragic true-life story of Arianrhod's son, Lleu Llaw Gyffes. It tells about the manner of his conception, his development as a boy, his youthful exploits in the company of Gwydion, his (Lleu's) wife (a stunning girl named Blodeuedd) and her buck of a lover, his (Lleu's) betrayal and exile as a man by transformation into an eagle, the usurpation of his land by the adulterer and executioner Gronw Bebyr, but vengeance comes, vengeance comes, and the story ends with the remarkable return of Lord Gyffes to rule prosperously over his *cantref*, the lands we now call Eifionydd and Ardudwy. And Gwydion meanwhile magicked Blodeuedd into an Owl (*don't* ask me how he did it!). He (Lleu) became King of Gwynedd in the end, we're abruptly told in a one-line medieval postscript. That's the plot. That's the story of Lleu Llaw Gyffes. That's the story of *Blodeuwedd*.

And so is begot an extremely complex genealogy of incest and rape and birth, the incredible conjurations of magicians, marriage, tragedy, personal loss, sexual proclivity, transmogrification, metempsychosis and nemesis and, clearly, the story is also, intriguingly, amongst all this, archaeological and onomastic. It is very firmly located in the landscape and in the place-names and the geography of Gwynedd, and it's this, this landscape link, this *territoriality*, as it happens, that interests the author. The story was once a part of the rich oral tradition of storytelling in Wales that is at least a millennium and a half old, and it is located, quite specifically, by name, by its place-names, in north-west Wales, in Gwynedd. Gwynedd in many ways is still today an unchanged *mythic* landscape. It *is* as old as the hills. It is Welsh. It is Welsh-speaking. The places that *The Mabinogion* identifies by name are still recognisable to us to visit today. And it is this connection, between landscape and myth, between the story and its place-names, between then and now, which holds the audience's attention throughout the telling of the story even today, suspending disbelief until, until the end (*Y Diwedd*). It happened. It happened, you see, *here*. In *this* place and *that* place, in Gwynedd. The names are printed on our modern Ordnance Survey maps made and published by the Ordnance Survey at Southampton. These places *exist*.

Metempsychosis. That's how this strange genealogy is largely begot. That early Celtic world was full of a belief in reincarnation as animals and undines and natural enchantment and astronomical omen and many magic ceremonies were celebrated each month in accordance with the date of the Druidic calendar and *place-names* in Wales had a mythical and mystical as well as a purely functional significance to them then. There is an indestructible and a defiant permanence about place-names in Wales which is a reflection of this peculiarly *Celtic* artefact of onomastic story-telling and with this naming craft goes, too, the parallel persistence and longevity of the language itself, the Welsh language, *Y Gymraeg*. It explains, in part, the language's completely unexpected survival over recent centuries (and its revival in recent decades). The names in Wales that are familiar to us now on maps and on signposts and on road-signs and in print, in publication, were known, also, some of them, *then*. Many of these Welsh place-names are well over a thousand years old. They are the impregnable folk-memory of that first in-migrating cult of Celts (*Y Cymry*) that came to *Cymru* (Wales) and told these stories in celebration of the deeds of the old Celtic gods, and a direct lineal descendant of this storytelling was *The Mabinogion*. Without these stories, most place-names in Wales would have been English'd out of Wales a long time ago.

There was no attempt (or necessity) then to distinguish between History and Myth but the topographic (the topo*nymic*) association was always made explicit by the storyteller (the *cyfarwydd*), whoever that monk was, and it is presented as such as a kind of geographical connection that runs throughout and makes sense of the clever entanglements of the story and its narrative. These, clearly, are important and historic places. And it doesn't really matter if it's history for real or if it's manufactured myth or if it's only a literary entertainment to occupy a dark night. The fact of the matter is that the heroes in this story – this magician, this cuckold, this seductress, this adulterer, this rapist, this sorceress – became quickly encapsulated into local legend like this by the telling and re-telling of this intricate tale and so entered, everlastingly, its place-names. They are alive today, these people, in the names of well-known topographical features in this particular part of Gwynedd. This is pre-Roman Welsh History. This is pre-Christian Myth. This is a Very Old Welsh Story. This is The Fourth Branch of The Mabinogi. It *happened*. It happened, you see, *here*, in Gwynedd, here in the upper left-hand corner of Wales. You can actually visit these legendary places even to this day if you like. You can still go to all the homes and haunts and courts and forts of these characters and it's all straight out of *The Mabinogion*. This book places you in the right direction.

The simplicity of the narration gives the story immediacy, dignity, pathos; and this is what makes the story historically objective, standing free of the anonymous narrator, distanced by its own independence and use of past tense, but linked, still, to the present, by a direct connection and that link is Welsh geography and Welsh topography. And it is these, in turn, that give the story its extraordinary *authenticity*. These places exist. Go to these places. You'll see what I mean.

The story is not only onomastic. It is implicitly, in places, also, erotic. You can sense this. You can feel this. But present-day written-down redactions of the original orally-told story only hint at that Welsh (and Irish) sense of sensuality and overtness of sexuality. I have tried to re-introduce an *occasional* element of explicit eroticism and sexual electricity into *my* rewritten anatomy of the accepted text. This, it turns out, is easy to do with an extravagantly seductive girl like Blodeuedd about.

This novel re-telling of the second part of The Fourth Branch of The Mabinogi, from a different angle, from a different emphasis, placing particular emphasis on developing its personalities and its eroticism and the motivation behind its complicated plot (the protagonists otherwise are rather *too* two-dimensional characters in *The Mabinogion*), is all part of what once used to be an accepted process (in the shadowy times before recorded History and Academic Writing began) of accretion and development and evolution in the oral tradition of telling a good story in Wales. This demanded of the travelling storyteller not only the memorisation of an extremely complicated story overheard but once from someone else, and the ability to give an accurate word-for-word repetition and an enthralling recitation of it to any gullible audience in Wales that would listen (and they did, they did, from *llys* to *llys*), but also the expectation was that this next recounting of it was going to add an unexpected elaboration, a further complication, a believable embellishment, a sudden extemporisation, and so on, like this, from *plas* to *plas*, from *din* to *dinas*, from *caer* to *castell*, from *cantref* to *cantref*, all the time. I'm only doing this, in this post-modernist text. It *wasn't* fixed. It wasn't even *written*. The story of Blodeuwedd, at first, was in the *oral* literary tradition. This is my contemporary attempt at the art. Speak it. *Listen* to it.

I play here the part not of dull scholarship but of the *Cyfarwydd*. I came here to mimic *The Mabinogion*, not to praise it. Sometimes I make it up. Sometimes I lie. I extemporise. I change. There are anachronisms. There are mistakes. There are mis-directions at some of the bilingual signposts. I make no apology for any of this. This story is, now, simply, a good *listen* is all. Though it must be said (I openly admit it) that in the twenty-first century (when it's published) the story of Blodeuwedd, as I re-tell it, the story has lost some of its, well its original 'aesthetic' sense. But I've added a lot more than I've taken away.

The source of the story that I have near at hand is an acknowledged classic and it's that recent definitive English translation of the eleventh-century Welsh manuscripts, made by Gwyn Jones and Thomas Jones of the University College of Wales at Aberystwyth, and the book is called (to continue to perpetuate the mistake) *The Mabinogion* (1949). It has been published over the decades in a succession of editions by Everyman, J.M. Dent, London, and was available as a recently revised paperback edition, on my desk, in my study, in that damp garreted cottage, on the right bank of the little Afon Beuno, in Y Bontnewydd, in Gwynedd, in late 1993. It took me two weeks to re-write it, seven years to get it done. This translation is the most authoritative and it's widely considered the best, I'm told. I have quoted from this scholarly work and mischievously *mis*-quoted it to add *some* verisimilitude and *some* authority to my adulterated text, quite often. It's too good a story to leave in the ill-lit and quiet library of academic pedantry. It requires a much wider readership than that. This is what I'm doing in re-telling it the way I do. I do *mock* pedestrian scholarship with ease and with jocularity. *Bugger* the professors! There you go. Sorry about that.

So, reader, learn to speak *The Mabinogion*. I recognise (of course) that pronunciation of many of the Welsh names may be a not insignificant problem for English-speaking readers. So without a lisp I list, below, generously, the approximate pronunciation of the main characters' names for reading out aloud, or to oneself, or to one's children, in everyday English, the story of *Blodeuwedd*:

Math	"Math"
Gwydion	"Gwid-Yon"
Arianrhod	"Are-Yan-Rhod"
Dylan	"Dull-ann"
Lleu Llaw Gyffes	"Thley Thlhow Guff-ess"
Blodeuedd	"Blod-dey-eth"
Gronw Bebyr	"Gron-oo Beb-urr"
Blodeuwedd	"Blod-dey-weth"

Math and Gwydion and Arianrhod and Dylan and Lleu Llaw Gyffes and Blodeuedd and Gronw Bebyr *et al* lived in Arfon ("Arr-von") and Eifionydd ("Avion-ith") and Ardudwy ("Arr-did, oo-we") a very long time ago yet even today we still call it Gwynedd ("Gwin-eth"). I suggest that you yourself go out and investigate the present-day places in Gwynedd where they once acted out *Blodeuwedd*. The *geography* of this story will have to be a separately-written guide book with all the unique six-digit grid reference numbers given, *in situ*, in its text. The constraint of limited space and the impracticality of easy integration of scholarly intercalary comment in *this* book and the *pusillanimity* of publishers (it has to be said) allows me to locate precisely only a few of the main legendary sites, in this book, in the list below, to guide you to go to these places at least:

Maen Dylan	SH 425 522
Caer Arianrhod	SH 423 547
Dinas Din-Lleu	SH 437 564
Castell Caernarfon	SH 478 627
Mur Castell	SH 706 387
Bryn Cyfergyr	SH 722 413
Clogwyn y Barcud	SH 543 532
Bryn y Castell	SH 726 429
Llyn Morwynion	SH 737 423
Llech Ronw	SH 716 405

To search out and research these places you will of course require a recent edition of an Ordnance Survey map (1:50 000 scale), an infallible ability to accurately navigate with that map, stout footwear, sandwiches, and wind-proof and water-proof clothing. (It rains a lot in Wales. There are lots of boggy bits. There are even, in some places, some *fatal* bits. Look what happens to unsuspecting women walkers on page 37! Take care, reader. Snowdonia is a pretty perilous playground.)

So there you have it. This is my book. This is my contrivance. Slim volume, eh? But there's *much* more to this story and to the landscape of North Wales than first attracts the visitor's glancing eye. There is (for example) (oh, you *will* find it), the language (*Y Gymraeg*); there's the History of Wales (*Hanes Cymru*); and there's Magic (*Cyfaredd*) and Myth (*Chwedl*). Welcome (*Croeso*) to Cymru (Wales). This is Gwynedd. These places exist. This is *The Mabinogion*. This is its gift.

So much by way of prologue and abbreviation and apology and preface. All this is but an introduction. I am about to begin. All hush, please. All quiet in the auditorium. Listen, ladies and gentlemen. *Listen.*

I begin my re-telling of *Blodeuwedd,* as follows:

BLODEUWEDD

The Beginning

Arianrhod, daughter of Dôn, is brought before Math the King, Math the Good, Math the Patriarch, Math the Courageous, Math the Oak-Hearted, Math, Math ap Mathonwy. And Math said:

— Maiden, is thy maidenhead intact?

— I know not other than that it is, hesistantly answers Arianrhod.

Math, not entirely convinced of the matter, insists that Arianrhod undertakes the test of virginity. King Math takes out his magic wand and manipulates it such that the rod becomes large, slightly bent, upright and red. He instructs Arianrhod:

— Sit astride this, young Arianrhod, and if thou art a maiden, well then, I shall know it.

Arianrhod does as she is told by Math but fails the test of virginity and drops out of her greatly distended, straining, vulva, a fine boy-child with a covering (a pelt, a pelage) of rich yellow hair. The boy, at birth, utters a bark at his new world and Arianrhod, in shame at the discovery of her lack of maidenhead, rushes still bleeding from the bloody birth to the door and drops a placental small something that trembles its neonatal grotesqueness on the brink of survival and death which Gwydion the Magician snatches up whilst all other eyes are riveted by the spectacle and the indecency of Arianrhod's first grief. Gwydion wraps the blood-soaked thing in a sheet of black silk and hides it in a small chest (an incubator), a settle, at home, at the base of his bed.

Math, in the practice as it then was of Welsh baptism, names the golden-haired new-born child thus:

— The name that I bestow upon this, this boy-child, is Dylan, said Math.

The moment that the boy was baptised like this, to everyone's astonishment, he, this chubby little chap, wobbles away, little arms flapping frantically, on his belly, and heads straightway to the nearest headland and, once there, immediately received the sea's nature and swam as well and more gracefully in it than even the best *pysgodyn* (fish) in the sea. And for that reason the boy thereafter was called Dylan.

The littoral site where this extraordinary event of the boy Dylan's entry into the sea took place and his transformation once there into a stream-lined mammalian sea-creature (Darwin himself could not have described it better) can be identified precisely as the headland known as Trwyn Maen Dylan on that curve of coast south of Caernarfon near Pontllyfni. The exact place is marked by a single exceptionally large boulder lying on the shingle and sand at the high-water mark of the beach and engraved into this stone, long ago, but now partly obscured by encrustation and the growth of green seaweed over it, is the boy's name, 'DYLAN'. This rock is still known on the map as Maen Dylan. It is an erratic in reality, dropped here by a retreating glacier at the end of the last great Ice Age, a long time in fact before Gwydion and Math.

Dylan, a child of an incestuous begetting, was half-man half-seal, a merman, part-man part-seal, a sea-creature, a phoco-*Homo*. Dylan means 'Sea-Son of Wave'. This is a very good name for a seal. Seal is *morlo* in Welsh and in Latin it's, it's *phoca*. Arianrhod's son Dylan abruptly became aquatic at Trwyn Maen Dylan and disappears equally as quickly from the rest of our story. That's the last we'll see of Dylan in *this* story.

The Boy

Gwydion the Magician was awakened one morning by a little cry that came out of the small wooden chest at the foot of his bed. He looks therein and in the folds of the jet-black sheet he finds an infant boy with bright yellow hair moving its arms about out of the swaddling. It seemed to Gwydion that there was something of his own likeness in the little face that looked up at him. Gwydion, with happiness in his heart and laughter in his eyes, takes this child up joyfully in his arms and goes out to seek a woman he knows in the nearby peasant settlement of Y Bontnewydd. She is a wet-nurse, a woman with breasts, as they used to say, a substitute mother with fullness of flow of lactation in her breasts, and she it is will nurse and comfort and give suckle to this darling little something that Gwydion's now unexpectedly got. She lives on a bank of the little *Afon Beuno* in a humble *croglofft* cottage they called 'New Lodge'. And Gwydion said:

– Take care of this boy for he is what makes my blood circulate and all the stars revolve and the seasons return.

That was smart. The child grows at a most remarkable rate. At the age of two, very precociously, he takes himself down the track that leads direct to King Math's Court at Caer Dathyl. Gwydion looks after him there and thereafter Gwydion it is attends to the boy's nurture and further development. Gwydion had read a book or two about Developmental Child Psychology when he was a postgraduate student in the Education Department at the University of York, so he was a good enough dad to the lad. And the boy grew accustomed to Gwydion and loved him better than anyone else. The fair-haired boy soon reached his fifth year and was as big then as a lad twice that age and strong with it too. Gwydion had recently taught the boy to whistle a mellow fluty tune like that of a blackbird's song and he, rather irritatingly, does not ever henceforward desist from this. Gwydion decides one day that it's about time for this boy to meet his procreatrix. Single parenthood, you see, is all very well but it's a very *time-consuming* occupation for a magician with other responsibilities and lots of domestic work and reams of writing to do. Gwydion takes hold of the prodigious lad's hand, and says to him seriously:

– There's someone I think you should meet.

Gwydion was Magician-in-Residence at Math's Great Court. Gwydion was garrulous. Gwydion was gregarious. Gwydion was a colourful character. He wore bright clothes. He laughed a lot. Gwydion was a chatterer. He told the strangest stories. He astonished his audiences with the audacity of his vitality and his play and invention. He was always active indoors and out. He collected seaweeds at the seashore and acorns in the woods. His illustrated lectures on Natural History and its link with Literature were invariably very entertaining. Gwydion was the best narrator of Tales in Wales. And Gwydion was also an Alchemist. Gwydion was a *Scientist*! Gwydion was *extraordinarily* busy. Too busy, you see, to be a father full-time and single-handed.

Gwydion took hold of the growing lad's hand and they walk purposefully, southwards, along the seashore.

– Where we goin', Dad?

– That isolated coastal castle in the distance that's named Caer Arianrhod. *That*'s where we're going, boy. And *don't* call me that.

The castle called Caer Arianrhod once stood at the edge of the sea on this shore south-west of Aber Menai where Gwydion and the boy walk but time and tide have combined with coastal erosion to take this place away today. It's been claimed by the sea. Caer Arianrhod now lies some distance out in Caernarfon Bay, sunk under the sea. But stand at the top of this mound called Dinas Din-Lleu and look in a direct line of sight straight out across the bay to the first *bwlch* just to the left of the end-most peak of Yr Eifl and there, out at sea, at very low tides, at spring tides, at vernal or autumnal equinox especially, you'll see, just above the swell, emerging there, not far away, about a mile away, you'll see out there a rocky crenulation arise, an oddly geometric arrangement of rocks, rocks that define the foundation of the battlement and tower and the sea-wall of this fortress, this sunken castle once called Caer Arianrhod. Caer Arianrhod today gives scaffold and sanctuary to teeming marine biology, and conger eels.

Arianrhod comes out to the iron-railing gate in the back-garden of Caer Arianrhod (with its gorse, stunted oak and hawthorn) to meet Gwydion (the rusty gate creaks) and Arianrhod greets him thus:

– *Sut dach chi*, Gwydion. What is this one that follows thee, this *bachgen* that whistles such sweetness of song like unto that of a blackbird?

– A son of thine is the boy.

Arianrhod is taken dramatically aback by this and then, as suddenly, angrily turns on Gwydion. Her words are full of anguish and there's a bitter resentment evident against her elder brother:

– What came over thee to put me to shame with uncle Math like that and to pursue that after-birth of my shame and to keep it incubated in thy laboratory as long as this?

– It is not a shame on you to claim as your own such a strong and handsome boy as this one is, Arianrhod.

– What is thy son's name, Gwydion?

'*Thy*' son. Arianrhod refuses to acknowledge the parenthood.

– There is as yet no name baptised on the boy, says Gwydion.

Arianrhod then, unexpectedly, pronounces three difficult destinies on the boy:

– He shall get no name until he get it from *me*. He shall not bear weapons until *I* myself equip him therewith. And thirdly, Gwydion, he shall *never* have for wife a mortal woman of the kind that now doth inherit this earth. Hark ye that cuckoo that calls in the distance? It is for that reason that I do this. To avoid the man's humiliation. Gwydion, I can *see* it.

The call of the cuckoo connotes cuckoldry. *Gwcw? Gwcw?* What *Cuculus canorus?* What *Cog?* Gwydion doesn't know what on earth she's talking about. Gwydion hears only the susurrant sound of the swash and the backwash of the waves that break at the stone base of Caer Arianrhod's protective sea-wall. This incessant sea. This constant sea. You'll see. Arianrhod's Castle was then at the very edge of the sea. Eventually it will succumb to the sea. *She* could probably see that inundation that happened in the future as well.

Arianrhod is being spiteful and angry, Gwydion thinks it to himself as he listens to the sound of the incoming sea, because she can never claim to be called maiden again ever since Math's maidenhead test was made public and that sea-creature Dylan came out of her. But Gwydion's got it completely

7

wrong. The woman in front of him is utterly repelled by the thought of the groping and the grabbing and the quick carnal intercourse so painfully is it inflicted by the manhood of all manner of men. And who can blame her that repulsion? She was sexually abused in childhood by her brother Gilfaethwy, raped openly by her uncle, racked with shame, emotionally drained, had become listless and, recently, anorexic. A constant nausea clutches at her vitals and lassitude and moroseness these days assail her. The reason is other than just discovery of loss of virginity, Gwydion. Arianrhod does not want a *husband*! You've got the wrong end of the woman's psychology, old man.

Arianrhod refuses to recognise the boy as her own and swears the three destinies on him in a vain attempt to obstruct his fate. She wants to protect him from the dark career and the disaster ahead which only she, Arianrhod, his mother, only she can see. But this seems rather odd to us because Arianrhod's prescience knows it as well as we do that she can *not* prevent it in the long run. Fate, once set in motion for this boy, is now, for her son, ineluctable. Arianrhod's lonely existence at Caer Arianrhod is marred, it seems, not only by a hatred of men and emotional emptiness but also by long periods of distress and confusion and what nowadays we would call a mental illness. Arianrhod's going psychiatric, sad to say. But the process of madness in those days gave glimpses into the Future as well and Arianrhod has a very clear picture of Blodeuedd gushing in bed with Gronw on page 21. Gwydion, of course, is as unaware as the reader is of the outcome of all this. Only Arianrhod knows.

Gwydion returns in a black temper to Caer Dathyl in Arfon with the boy he's got who's not yet got a name. Magic and trickery and cunning and disguise will now be required to release the boy from his mother's three curses and Gwydion must act at this quick. The very next morning Gwydion collects from the seashore at Aber Menai thallus and frond of Dulse and Carragheen and Bladder-Wrack and Saw-Wrack and Flat-Wrack and Channel-Wrack and Laver and Sea-Girdle and out of these seaweeds he fashions a ship. Don't ask me how he did it. And the name of the ship was the *Gwymon*. He sets sail in this vessel with the boy on board and they are in the semblance of a shoe-maker and his young apprentice. They approach the seaward side of Caer Arianrhod and anchor in its shallow bight. Arianrhod is tempted by the goodness of look and the texture of the leather and the uncommon colours used to tan the skin so that no one has ever seen leather more lovely in colour and comfort than this. She goes out to the *Gwymon* in order that precise measurements can be taken by this master craftsman to shape for her a low-heeled, nice-looking, lady's shoe with golden pigmentation upon the strap and the leather maroon, *os gwelwch yn dda*, my foot size is 4½ or possibly 5. A wren (*Troglodytes troglodytes*) happens to alight on the gunnel of the ship just as Gwydion engages himself in cutting out the leather. The boy, leaving off his work of stitching the strips in place, yet not discontinuing his whistling, aims a tiny grain of sand at the wren, throws it and hits the wren, exactly, between the thinnest sinew of its spindly leg and its littlest, its most brittlest bone (its tarsus)! Arianrhod is absolutely amazed by the accuracy of the hit and can only comment (in difficult Welsh):

– This fair one's a skilfully deft hand!

– That's it, announces Gwydion (though not exactly pleased with 'it'). The boy's acquired his name from thee as thou said it should be. The name he has from now on in his life is this name: Lleu Llaw Gyffes.

At that, the shoe-work vanished back into a tangle of Kelp and Thongweed and Oarweed and Bootlace-Weed and Knot-Wrack and Bladder-Wrack and Tangle and Gwydion took on his own aspect as did the boy. Arianrhod was very angry at Gwydion's deception. *And* she didn't get to get a new pair of fashionable ladies' shoes. She'd have to go instead to Stead & Simpson, or Jones the Bootmaker, in Bangor.

Lleu Llaw Gyffes, then, is the lad's name from now on in the story. '*Lleu*' is fair and '*Llaw*' is one-hand and '*Gyffes*' is dab or adept or nimble or skilful or deft. Lleu Llaw Gyffes. Fair-Hand-Adept. Daft name really. But that's how he got it. There you go. Some parents choose the names of their children as carelessly as that.

The next deception arranged by Gwydion was for them both to arrive at Caer Arianrhod in the disguise of two young bards travelling from Pen-y-bont in the Vale of mid-Glamorgan who called themselves Iolo and Ogmore Morgannwg. They came to Caer Arianrhod over Bryn Arien and Cefn Clun Tyno by way of Gorad Beuno. Arianrhod, not suspecting that anything was amiss in this, again, lets them in and, well, to hasten the telling of this slow part of the story, she arms Lleu with warrior's weapons because of the nearby commotion and clamour of an attacking Irish fleet that she thinks is thick upon the deep (but this illusion of the mustering of maritime marauders' ships at the entrance to the sea-gate of Caer Arianrhod has been conjured up from out of Gwydion the Magician's imagination and is not real at all). Irishmen in those days had an occasional reputation in the Llŷn for pillage and rape in this vulnerable peninsula of Wales and Arianrhod had had enough of *that*. Arianrhod quickly gives Lleu the weapons to defend them. The second curse on Lleu is thus quite easily overcome. Gwydion congratulates himself in Latin: QED, *Quod Erat Demonstrandum*. Arianrhod was furious at the success of Gwydion's second trick and kicks him out of Caer Arianrhod (she'd bought herself a pair of blue Doc Martens' boots). Gwydion, with Lleu in hand, hastens to run away along the shore and, laughing, they head homeward toward Aber Menai. Arianrhod, less hysterical now, shouts after him:

– The *third* is too great a condition for *thy* magic alone to unlock it.

Gwydion stops laughing at the sound of that. He is all too aware of his own limitations. He'll have to go to Math.

So, the boy has now got a name, daft though it is, and weapons and arms and warrior's equipment and, of course, naturally, in those days, a horse. An *Equus. Equus caballus*. A mustang taken from remote Cwm Caseg deep inside the Carneddau. A direct descendent it is of the truly wild Przewalski horses of Inner Mongolia and China! It's a fine-looking Welsh Mountain Pony anyway. But; and here's the rub. He's not yet got a *wife* to mount. This worries Gwydion.

Lleu, by now, had grown up fast into a very strong lad who is perfect in his features and in his stature is as a man. A very handsome and fair-haired Welsh lad he most certainly was, but intellectually, well, it has to be admitted, a bit slow, a bit *twp* was Lleu. A bit bird-brained really. The lad had not a lot of intelligence. He'd have been a really good rugby-player for Wales if the game had been invented then. *That* kind of Neanderthal Welshman, if you understand what I mean. Still, never mind, Gwydion did the best he could for Lleu and brought him up according to the books he'd read and Gwydion had the Architect at Math's Court construct for them both a great stronghold for them both to reside in. The fort was a wooden construction built on top of an existing great earthwork near Aber Menai which overlooked Caernarfon Bay, as it still does today. Today, a local estate agent like Gwyn Roberts would probably describe Gwydion's new property thus:

> Detached double-fronted traditional Celtic Wooden Fort extended at the back to include a cottage. Elevated site enjoying unrestricted views of Caernarfon Bay, Holyhead Mountain and, on a clear day, as far as the Wicklow Hills in Ireland. Small paddock of nine acres and a stable-cum-workshop used as a summer cottage, together with other useful outbuildings. Hall, living-room, kitchen, lounge, and study/laboratory, bathroom/toilet, 2 bedrooms, front belvedere and a bench. Further details on request. Offers in excess of £199,000.

And Gwydion named their new home 'Din Lleu'.

Din Lleu is known to us today as Dinas Din-Lleu, or Dinas Dinlle (The Stronghold-Position of the Fortified House of Lleu Llaw Gyffes and Gwydion). This is an immense mound which is now slipping and sliding and crumbling in days of gales and rainy weather, quite badly, into the sea. (It rains a lot in Wales.) The sea-facing side is constantly being eroded by the prevailing wind and pounded by salt-laden sea-spray and waves at high-water. Half of it's gone already but it is, still, a very impressive earthwork.

The mound is not man-made though the Romans adapted it to make it into a ring-fort. It is a *geomorphological* feature, an isolated hillock of glacial drift, a terminal moraine, the only hump on this otherwise notably dull and dreary coastline and it is remarkable. The views from Din Lleu of the Rivals (Yr Eifl) and Gyrn Ddu and Gyrn Goch and Bwlch Mawr are unrivalled and for backdrop there's the Nantlle Ridge and a panorama of most of the snow-covered 3,000-foot mountains of Wales. Caer Arianrhod is not far away (already said) and from Din Lleu you can clearly see Maen Dylan.

Din Lleu was the place where Lleu Llaw Gyffes was brought up through gawky adolescence into early manhood in the care and the custody of Gwydion.

It's said that Lleu Llaw Gyffes was, by now, the most handsome-looking young bachelor-man that any mortal woman is ever likely to set lascivious eyes on. But Lleu had a problem. He couldn't. He just couldn't. Lleu was… Lleu was…, impotent. There, I've said it. The man on him shrivelled up into naught at even the thought of taking a maiden that was still intact as a maiden to act it out in bed as his wife. Gwydion knew that Arianrhod's third curse was the cause of this embarrassment and the lad's continued celibacy and the curse of it *had* to be broken. Difficult one this, even for a magician as accomplished as Gwydion. So Gwydion went to Math. Math, it seems, knew quite a lot about the misbehaviour of one's manhood like this. It was known that he (Math) had had employment of a *troedawc* (a curious quirk) and other devices and contrivances instead of the intercourse of wives for just this same kind of problem. Perhaps he could help.

The Manufacture of A Wife

Gwydion, flicking his coat-tail as was his manner, made to Math the most sustained complaint in the world against Arianrhod and that third curse she'd cursed upon Lleu. He, Gwydion, just couldn't counter the spell. He'd lost countenance enough in public already. The girls in the streets of Caernarfon and the waifs down at Cei Llechi, the quay, had even got to know about it. Math said:

– Well, well, who would'st have known that flaccidity of cock afflicted a well-built lad like Lleu when brought to the attention of a maiden. I, too, I have known *occasional* impotence on me. I've had *that* embarrassment. Poor Lleu. We'd better do something about this and quick, Gwydion. Yes. We'll make him a… an unusually attractive, yes, by cunning stunt, Gwydion, we'll make him a… a *stunning* maiden. No ordinary maiden, mind you. We'll make him an extraordinary maiden to take as his wife, not mortal, but made out of… out of… out of *blodau*! Flowers! Petals! That's it! That ought to undo thy sister's trick. He'll get his way that way, you'll see. We'll make him a far better wife than mere mortals manufacture themselves by that messy business of theirs of slipping insemination and nine months' gravidity. Let's do it then. Gwydion, get thee thy cloak.

Math dons his gown. Gwydion gets his cloak.

Math's gown is dark green with a gloss sheen and it is embroidered all about with the swirls and loops and curves and the corrugations of what look like the leaves and acorns of Oak. Gwydion's cloak is a warm brownish buff in general appearance but in places it's brightly coloured with blue and white patches and black on the wing, white at the tail, with a hood, when erected, streaked black and white and with a moustache-like black streak at its rim. All is got ready. The two magicians, ceremoniously clad like this, enter the central Laboratory. They betook them to their Arts and began to display their Magic, though today we'd call it 'Science'.

King Math and Gwydion work to combine and concentrate their powers of imagination and magic and knowledge of electricity and Botany and by their conjurement and alchemy and with the freshly collected flowers of Oak and the flowers of Meadowsweet and the flowers of Broom added to this and that sparking and simmering flask and crucible and alembic and retort, they, somehow, called forth, out of this apparatus and a bubbling copper cauldron, they procreated (by recombinant DNA technology, probably) the fairest and most sexually appealing young maiden that mortal man has ever clapped his eye on. And they named her **Blodeuedd**.

The flowers of Oak (*Derwen*) and the flowers of Meadowsweet (*Blodau'r Mêl*) and the flowers of Broom (*Banadlen*) required by the two cloaked wizards to manufacture the maiden are commonly found in the local Welsh countryside in spring and mid-summer. The plants are indigenous hereabouts in hedges and in ditches and in lanes around Llandwrog, Llanfaglan, Y Bontnewydd and Clynnog Fawr.

The slender pale-green tassel-like catkins (the male flowers) and the tiny axillary greenish-white (female) flowers of the Sessile Oak (*Quercus petraea*) bloom between April and June as do the bright golden-yellow flowers of Broom (*Cytisus scoparius*) whilst the numerous creamy-white flowers which make up the frothy heads of the spikes of the sweetly-scented Meadowsweet

(*Filipendula ulmaria*) flower between June and September. We can thus rather exactly *date* the collection of these flowers which Math and Gwydion needed immediately for their distillation. The three species are in bloom simultaneously *only* in mid-June. So, Blodeuedd must have been made on or about the sixteenth day, let's say, of June. This mid-summer's day is the day of her birth-day! It was a Thursday. Blodeuedd means 'Flowers' (she is the 'Flower-Maiden') and 'Flowers' is 'Blooms'. And that is why June 16th is known to this day in Welsh literary circles as 'Bloomsday'.

Math and Gwydion were completely knackered after that. But look at her! She is exceptionally beautiful to behold. She has a stunningly good figure. She is slim. She is slender. She is small-breasted still. She is only just sixteen. She is at the height of her nubility. She's ready already. Her nymphancy is over. She has tawny-coloured hair. She has black owl-like eyes. She is enchanting to look at. She's seductive. She has susceptibly thin shoulders and the nape of her neck arches, and aches to be kissed. Oh! Look at this! Look what Math and Gwydion the Magicians have created! She's so shevelled and kempt, she's full of ept and's got heaps of ert. And her name is Blodeuedd! Wow! She's as pretty as, as the flowers she's made out of! (Blodeuedd is as pretty as your mother was when *she* was fifteen.) Blodeuedd, all say it, Blodeuedd is the most beautiful girl in the Western World! Lleu and Blodeuedd slept together that night.

(Truly, Gwydion the Magician moves in mysterious ways his wonders to perform.)

And they both lived happily ever after...

But Lleu, to his eternal shame that night, was still but as a boy next morning. Lleu remained untouched. Lleu stayed chaste. This is. This is the best-kept secret of *The Mabinogion*. It happened like this. Blodeuedd had said, in bed:

– You must not aim to part my legs one from the other, Llaw Gyffes, for they shall altogether and unconditionally remain together. Because

15

between them I have a snug little nest where maidens' fingers have a tendency to play and it is not seemly for thee to see me at it nor yet for thee to prick me.

Lleu doesn't realise that she's telling him this to tease him with this in preparation thereafter to please him with this! He is unable to. Can't get it to. He sulks. He is unheld and unenveloped that night. He sleeps eventually. Lleu is such a daft twat.

King Math, who does not know the truth of the situation between the young couple, and they do not tell it, gives to Lleu and Blodeuedd a gift in celebration of the assumed night's consummation of the marriage and this endowment to Lleu and his wife is the *cantref* called Cantref Din-odyn equivalent in extent to that part of Gwynedd known then as now as Eifionydd ('Eifynydd') and Ardudwy. It included Cantref Gwaelod. This is Lleu's first possession of Welsh territory. He will lose it. He will reclaim it. We, like Lleu, will later come back to it.

A *cantref* was a territorial area of land in Wales that contained a hundred homesteads and this territory was usually divided amongst two or three local lords or kings or athelings into smaller regions so that each in his *llys* had his own landlordship over that individual part or commote (*cwmwd*). *Cantrefi*, the plural, means, literally, a 'hundred townships'. The *tref* or township was not a cluster of houses grouped together as the name would imply to a city gent but was simply a division of the countryside across which rather isolated Welsh farmsteads straggled. Lleu was greatly honoured by that covenant from King Math. Lleu had the *whole cantref*! Lleu had the whole lot. Math, perhaps, suspects that Lleu is his (Math's) son and not necessarily only Gwydion's own incubation.

Lleu and Blodeuedd went into Caernarfon to the office of the Agent of the Land and Estates of Arfon and Eifionydd and Ardudwy and chose as a property for their habitation and comfort a residence in the northern uplands of Ardudwy overlooking a lake. And this court of theirs (this *llys*) was called Llys Mur Castell.

Llys Mur Castell is known to us today as Tomen y Mur. The name is in reference to a conspicuous feature, a prominent mound, looking exactly like a Norman *motte*, a bump on an otherwise flat area of exposed and weather-swept hillside, situated on a spur of Mynydd Maentwrog. The evidence all round on the ground is that the Romans had for a long time occupied the place. Tomen y Mur overlooks a lake. That lake today is called Llyn Trawsfynydd though King Math had named it Llyn Maentwrog.

Mur Castell was a house-fort and small court (a '*walled castle*') where Lleu and Blodeuedd lived in great style and comfort even though they did not then have nuclear-generated electricity. The climate of course was much more genial then than it is now and times were a lot happier than the bleak impression we get there today, driving up there today, of wind-swept isolation and treelessness and the grey and gloomy Rhinogydd Hills blocking the western horizon and the long expanse of marsh and reed which undulates away as very uninviting moorland to the south and to the east and the cold and the wet and the dark rain-clouds that now come louring in from a bleak south-westerly direction. Mur Castell, *then*, was a very *nice* place for our couple to inherit as their home in the northern uplands of Ardudwy. Mur Castell was a very desirable residence in those Celtic times when things were remarkably different then. Something *bad* has happened since to this landscape and to our environment. You can sense this. You can see this. Just go up there to Tomen y Mur in the rain today and look down on that *waste-land* below you with sheep and the concrete blocks of a decommissioned Nuclear Power Station and the lines of electricity pylons.

The newly-married couple arrive at Mur Castell and a retinue of handmaidens came with them too to attend to Blodeuedd's every desire and Lleu Llaw Gyffes ruled considerately and kindly and with good judgement and justice over all his people in the *cantref* of Eifionydd and Ardudwy. Everyone, more or less, was happy. That's the way it should be. The story *should* end here. 'And they both lived happily ever after'. *That's* what's usually written in true-love stories with satisfactory and romantic endings. But it *doesn't* end here for Lleu Llaw Gyffes, does it, on page 17. Because Fate. Forget ye not thy fate, Lleu, known only to your mother. Arianrhod has faded away from the telling of this tale with onset of madness and anorexia nervosa and Blodeuedd, thy manufactured wife, has now become the central character. Time ticks on to catastrophe, Lleu. Beware the end of October.

Here Comes The Cuckold!

Lleu went away one fine day, in August, whistling away to his heart's content, on horseback, through country lanes lined with hawthorn and oak and bracken and bilberry and gorse and foxglove and all the moors are in full bloom with all the cross-leaved heath and the heather that's out. It's August 21st. Lleu has arranged to visit Math his benefactor and Gwydion his teacher back at the Great Court called Caer Dathyl in Arfon or Castell Caernarfon as we now call it, with its town, its wall and its quay, situated at the mouth of the River Seiont.

Lleu Llaw Gyffes has gone elsewhere, to a meeting, a conference with Math and Gwydion. Blodeuedd is at Llys Mur Castell alone at last with her handmaidens and they are all eager to occupy the occasion by unhitching themselves of their intricate stitch and taut shift-straps. What a bother this bodice-work is! The bra had not yet been invented. There is not a fresh of breath air on this hot summer's day. The sun burns blindingly bright, a great orb of heat high in the scorched sky. There is not a cloud about, cumulus, nimbus, cirrus or otherwise. The heat on the day has silenced even the skylark's towering flight and its song is not sung on the moorland. All is too hot. All is silence. All is expectant. A heat haze is on the heather. The heathers in bloom. The day's a daze with the heat and the haze and it's not yet mid-day. All yes take yes their under yes things off. Then. What's this? Oh, oh. Here comes *Fate*. A great male Red Deer, *Cervus elaphus*, an antlered stag, suddenly appears and staggers past the window where Blodeuedd without a stitch on is stretched at full stretch and caressed is her breast and with moistened finger she has placed in position her hand to play and it leaps

18

as best it can in the circumstances across the hot moors and hills leading northwards and close at heel to the nearly exhausted ungulate came a pack of stag-hounds and huntsmen on horse and on foot swearing and cursing at the stag's endurance and apologising to their lord for their profanities and blasphemy and any other unexpurgated bad language he might have overheard and, quick as they'd all come, they'd gone. But Blodeuedd had seen *him*. Strong thighs he has on him and his back was straight and his buttocks bounced and his muscles bunched as he urged on the strong stallion under him. She could imagine the similar thrust and thrust and thrusts of. Good fantasy that to have. The mounting. The motion. The motion; the motion. Slow. Slow now. Slow down now. The moment. The moment comes!

– Yeeeeeeeeeeeeeeeeeeeeeeeeeeeeeeeeeeeeeeeeeeeeeess!!! whispered Blodeuedd.

Curious she was to. With her it was not as with other wives that will and would and want and wait but never do. So she sent a messenger to find out the name of the lord who hunted the stag and gave invitation to this buck to rest his body and come to sip a cup of Ty-phoo Tea with her at Llys Mur Castell. It's come all the way by a ship called a clipper (the *Cutty Sark*) from China or Ceylon or Sri Lanka as we now know it. We also serve wholemeal date and walnut scones (with butter, jam and cream) from the Tea-House (Tŷ Te) called 'Caffi Cwrt' at Cricieth (proprietors Irene and Sioned Roberts). My husband is absent. I have been left all alone. Come hither, Hunter, for afternoon tea. RQSVP, she wrote at the bottom of the invitation card. *Respondez* Quickly *Si'l Vous* Please. Wales was bilingual, you see, even then.

The man was Gronw Bebyr, Lord of Penllyn, and the *cantref* he had was to the south and west of Llyn Tegid. These are the lands we now call the Arans and the Arennigs.

Blodeuedd hears the sound of the creak of the entrance-gate opening and Gronw Bebyr the Huntsman approaches the heavy oak door. Blodeuedd runs fleet-foot down the wooden steps of the winding staircase in the Tower of Llys Mur Castell to meet him. She opens the door. Gronw at first sight of her is immediately in thrall of her, and says:

– We caught the Red Deer over at Cynfael River and I with my own sword have slain it. My lady, its antlers, from recent rutting, here is its antlers and this horn is for thee. Accept this trophy as quickly as I will now accept as quick, now that I see the radiance that is on thee, I'll gladly accept; thy kind invitation. Let us together then; have a cream tea.

Blodeuedd looked on him and the moment she looked on him her skin it did suffuse with warmth for him and her vulva became warm and humectate and wet. She smiled, self-consciously, crossing her redolent legs, and said to Gronw:

– Yes, yes, I will, Oh *Yes*.

What *was* she saying? Blodeuedd was tingling all over. She was electrified with thoughts of dangerous propinquity. She felt, very suddenly, very sexually aroused. And Gronw? Gronw, what with the excitement of the stag-hunt and the kill and the heat of the day and now the allurement of this captivatingly beautiful young woman in front of him in the full bloom of her youth who wore a chestnut-brown pleated (or is it brinded) light cotton summer dress (size 12) from Etam with a floral-print design of somehow quite familiar-looking flowers and an occasional tantalising glimpse when she moved like that to laugh like that, of... oh!, of awfully pretty white stitchery from Debenhams underneath (Gronw Bebyr, it will be revealed, has a propensity for ladies' underwear) and her waist and her tawny-coloured crimped hair down to her breast and her legs and her bare feet and the smooth ankle she has and her wide-opened eyes, such that he (Gronw) can not resist coquettish femininity such as this and the pungent scent of her sexuality and the enticement of the accoutrements of her gender and also, anyway, he can not conceal that he loved her (he has an enormous erection on him which she can not help but admire and stare), and so he told her so:

– My lady, Mrs Gyffes, let us engage in thy bed.

– Yes, oh yes, I want thee to and I to swive thee too. *Yes*!

And straightway they embraced and went to bed and engaged at it quick. Let us apply an eye to that keyhole at Llys Mur Castell. Blodeuedd was passionate, spontaneous, amusing, inventive, extravagantly articulate and very erotic in just her black stockings in bed with Gronw. She is not oblivious to the fact that one day this extra-marital affair, this love-making, this summer's day fucking, *this*, one day, would be celebrated in Welsh literature. She was *shockingly* pornographic. In earthquaking, noisemaking, succussatory intercourse they fuckfuckfuckfuckfuckfuck fucked. It was a very hot afternoon. And when at last they did disengage from this, they talked enthusiastically about the love and affection and lust at first sight they'd conceived one for the other, and, so saying, urgently they did do it again and again in this same intense and frank manner, nine times in all, till sleep came upon them as eventually it must even to the most ardent and energetic and athletic of lovers. This was better than all the frigging she'd ever done in the company of her handmaidens and that same finger-play which Blodeuedd had had to do before sleep because Lleu couldn't do anything like *that* that this Gronw had just done. Wow! And so contented, sleep befell unfaithful Blodeuedd. An owl outside the bedroom window went '*tu-whit, tu-whooo*', but neither the reader nor Blodeuedd understands as yet the significance of this signal.

Next day she requested Gronw to stay for another night of love that was so deep and pressing and penetrative. She could keep this kind of thing going for hours on end if *he* was up to it too. She'd, yes, had many a multiple what-do-you-call-it mucositease like this before but only with her hand and handmaidens in games of girlish practice that cannot compare with this. This was more, more satisfactory. Please, she said. All right, said Gronw. Gronw stayed the second night (her legs were wide open and her shaggy placket exposed and all inverecund like this she lay there) and seven engagements they had of each other.

Next day Blodeuedd again begged Gronw to stay for yet one more night and, this time, promises:

– And on the morrow of this night, I shall let thee go.

Gronw acquiesces (and what man wouldn't) though by now he was sore in shaft and sorely troubled in mind by the thought of the risk he was taking

21

in agreeing to this arrangement if, for example, her absent husband (where *was* he?) should happen to return home unexpectedly the next morning and find him (Gronw Bebyr) having not only bed & breakfast but breakfast in bed with Blodeuedd his wife! *She* was insatiable. Gronw stayed the third night and three engagements they had of each other.

And in the morning Blodeuedd said:

– You can go now, Gronw, but I for my part want more of that big part of thee to enter it up into me.

– Myself, too, I feel this for thee, said Gronw.

There was no counsel for them both other than to get rid of the incumbent husband if they were serious about staying together forever and ever as each had vowed to each the other in the importunity of their love-making in the heat and the sweat and the convulsion of those moments in between the cambric sheets of Blodeuedd's unmaid bed. There were crumbs in the bed. A thought crosses her mind:

– I'd better wash this bed-sheet lest Lord Gyffes detect the stain of another's cuckoldry into me and that moistening which from me also hath so profusely dripped.

– Look, my love, my petal, my beautiful flower, my Blodeuedd, says Gronw (Lleu, you see, never said anything as romantic as *that* to his wife and that's the main part of his problem). Find out the way that his death might be brought about. Do this under pretence of caring for him. Speak closely to him. Draw forth from him how his death can be dealt.

– I'll find it out of him. This will be for us, Gronw, and because, well, because, because I want thy cock up inside me again. Go now, Gronw. Take this contrivance, if you must, to remember me by.

They have suspected, as we have done too, that Lleu, for all his failing as a man unable to man a maiden in bed, is nevertheless quite inviolate in his innocence and protected from mortal harm by some kind of complicated charm administered no doubt by his guardian Gwydion. Gronw departs. He has a suspender belt and a pair of black stockings in a side pocket of his kirtle. Gronw will grow and groan at home in this. What a contrivance! (But, then

22

again, I guess it all depends on what turns you on.)

Lleu comes back from Caer Dathyl in Arfon into Ardudwy later that same day. He doesn't suspect anything. None of the maidens who collect the resonant linen from Blodeuedd's bedroom *dare* tell him. Poor Lleu Llaw Gyffes. Cuckolded by his neighbour. Lleu, the daft twat, doesn't even notice the new pair of stag's antlers in pride of place above his own hearth. Poor Lleu.

The Betrayal

That night Lleu and Blodeuedd went to bed together but Blodeuedd tonight does not talk to him as it is her usual wont with him in bed.

– What ails thee, my wife, that thou art stuck for a story to tell, enquires Lleu.

– My concern and loving care for thee, dearest husband mine, is this. If thou were to, to go sooner to the Underworld, Hades, or Hell as some now call it, than I, what then would I, a young widow bereft and left all alone in this world, unprotected from other men's advances at night, what then would I *do* without you?

Lleu laughs:

– It is not very easy to slay me according to the advice of my tutor, the magician Gwydion.

– Tell me! Tell me how then thou might be slain. For it is known throughout Wales that the best remembrancers are not of thy gender but mine and I, a woman, thy wife, I will make doubly sure then to avoid the circumstances set out for thee. My memory in this matter is a much surer safeguard than thine. Tell me, Lleu. *Tell* me.

Lleu then lists the impossible conditions learnt in a litany from Gwydion and against which Arianrhod, his mother, by setting three curses upon her son, had laboured in vain to protect him from this very same destiny:

– Only when smitten through by a spear that has taken the maker a year

23

to make on Sabbath days when other goodly folk are out at Mass. Cannot be slain within a building, nor yet outside a house. Cannot be slain on horseback, nor yet when out on foot. Cannot be slain on water, nor on dry land. Only when a warm cauldron has been prepared for me as bath, beside a river-bank, with a thatched frame in half-vault over this tub, and a billy-goat present so that I have placed one foot on the back of this *bwch gafr* or *Capra hircus* as Gwydion calls it and the other on the rim of the aforementioned cauldron he said. Whosoever should smite me with that ungodly spear when I am arranged as an acrobat precariously thus, in these special circumstances only, then it is he, and he alone, that can bring about my death.

Lleu laughs at the end of the list, though a little nervously this time we suspect, and says:

– Methinks it's nigh on impossible to accomplish it, isn't it, Blodeuedd, to bring all these quite bizarre pre-conditions about?

– Yes, Lleu. Yes. I think we can manage I mean avoid all that. *Nos da.*

Nos da? This is the first night in his marriage that Lleu has not had to listen to a good night story in bed with Blodeuedd who was *always* at it. Lleu really is an innocent. Poor Lleu.

Lleu is a hero of the type who can only be killed under certain seemingly impossible conditions. The theme is a common one in Celtic myth. It sustains narrative interest in a story. We know that Lleu will die, we know that his murder is apparently impossible, and yet, and yet we wait, we listen attentively, to see how the incredible arrangement is to be stage-managed by the storyteller and how the death of the man can be accomplished. Lleu's secret of apparent invulnerability has been drawn out of him by Blodeuedd under importunity of love for him and from now on in the story Lleu's predestined fate is absolutely unavoidable and it is imminent (we know this from other plots and plays). The arrangement needed to bring about his death is intriguingly very complex and naturally we want to know now how can it be done. *That's* the storyteller's trick. We want to *know*. (Tell! Tell! Tell me all about! I want to know all about!) The narrator is well aware of the device and plays upon this element of our natural curiosity and expectation and we, the listeners, the readers, suspend our disbelief. We anticipate the outcome and yet we hope that it is wrong. That's 'fate' for you. There's *tragedy* for you.

There is a third theme that has been introduced quite quietly and subtly at this point in the telling of the story and it is this: the theme of being between two worlds where things are neither this nor that. We are about to enter a surreal and very pagan realm of duality and magic and superstition. We, like Lleu, are on the edge not only of our seats in the auditorium. We are situated on the brink, it seems, of somewhere in between a roaring waterfall and a calm pool; sunshine and shade; death and reincarnation; this world and the Otherworld; Life and Death; life and, and Insanity. The fabric of reality for Lleu Llaw Gyffes, and for the reader, is about to be ripped apart.

(And by the way; never trust a woman made out of flowers.)

Blodeuedd communicates her knowledge of the fatal conditions to her lover Gronw Bebyr, and he, in his infatuation and lust to have her partly undressed again, labours for a year in a secret forge (normally closed on Sundays) in the making of just the right kind of arrow (I mean spear). He dreams every night about her dresses and things and underthings on an endless clothes-line of possession in ceaseless repetition and bliss. He dwells each day, each unoccupied afternoon, on the autoerotic touch of her 10-denier black stockings under uplifted skirt with a hand on his cock. Gronw is a. (A voice inside his head is saying: Vengeance will come! Vengeance *will* come!) Then, at last, finished at the forge, Gronw sends the fateful signal from the General Post Office in the High Street in Bala first thing on Monday morning:

ARROW MANUFACTURED. READY TO DO THE
DEED THAT MUST BE DONE. AWAITING FURTHER
INSTRUCTION. YOURS, IN SUSPENSE,
G.B.

None at Llys Mur Castell except Blodeuedd alone can understand the meaning of the enigma of the arrival of the telegram which had come out of the blue from Bala. Blodeuedd, in secret, writes out the instruction that Gronw must now follow to the letter, seals the treacherous message with moistened second finger, a kiss from from her lips, and sends it, in an envelope marked 'Private & Confidential', first class, by the very next post, from the Post Office in Llan Ffestiniog, a village not far away from Llys Mur Castell. And this is the gist of the letter that is addressed to Gronw:

> Await with thy spear under cover of the hill called Bryn Cyfergyr that overlooks Cwm Cynfael and Cynfael River and, once in position there, look south-west to that blood-stained spot on the bank of the small brook called Afon Bryn Saeth, where last summer thou didst slay that stag, because *there*, later this year, at that spot, on the eve of *Nos Calan Gaeaf*, I will have arranged my *in*adequate husband, ludicrously, as is his destiny, as thy target. *Do* it. Yours, urgently. Yours, openly. Desperately wanting it,
>
> Blodeuedd

(Nasty bit of work *she*'s turning out to be.)

Blodeuedd attracts the attention of Lleu one day with her ingratiation and solicitation and feminine play and, in so doing, touching him, persuades her unsuspecting husband to demonstrate that absurd arrangement he has to get himself into, oh, you remember, Gwydion's list you told me about last year, if I make ready a goat got from the Great Orme and the thatch and a tin bath by a brook and:

– I'll make it thy *bridal* bath, said Blodeuedd.

She always did have the owlish way with that look of her large black eyes and that seductress's lift of one of her eyebrows. And anyway, in his present condition (in this anticipatory circumstance), how could Mr Gyffes resist? Of course he couldn't! This is going to be *it*, thought Lleu. Tonight's the night! Arianrhod's third curse on me will be undone tonight! How was it that I could not look upon her petals before this? Lleu prepares himself for the bath and the bride.

We find Lleu, in due course, later that same day, on the eve of the Night before the Winter Calend, trustingly perched, demonstrating the fact of the absolutely impossible, with one foot on the back of a white Kashmiri he-goat and the other foot on the edge of a red metal tub, rather unsteadily, under a half-canopy of green thatch, whistling out loud that loud fluty song of his, with a huge I mean huge erection on him at last, having just had a warm bath, looking rather flushed, completely naked, on a bank of a tributary of the Cynfael River across the moor from Llys Mur Castell, above Bont Newydd, near the village of Llan Ffestiniog. Blodeuedd's in the background. I hear the cry of the audience at once all say:

– Oh Jaysus, Lleu, get thee quickly away!

Ah, but now 'tis too late and too distant to warn Lleu. Fate, you see. Fate is about to catch up with our friend Lleu. Gronw Bebyr, with arrow in hand, rises up from under cover of that crag nearby called Bryn Cyfergyr …

The source of the remarkable Afon Cynfal (the Cynfael River) lies at Llyn y Dywarchen high on the bleak open moors of the bog-lands of Y Migneint east of the little village of Llan Ffestiniog. This moorland stream (the Afon Cynfal) suddenly changes its character near Pont yr Afon Gam (the location, at 1,255ft, of the highest petrol station and café in Wales it used to be but it's closed down now, the place is up for sale) as it plunges, very dramatically, down a precipitous 400-foot cleft of a gorge in a series of six or seven cascades forming the splendid and vigorous waterfall called Rhaeadr y Cwm which is rather uninspired and too bland a name for so great and dramatic a waterfall as this. This is a two-faced fall. Throughout most of the day, except for a short period, one side of the ravine will always be in deep shadow. Photographers can not adequately capture Rhaeadr y Cwm. Too much contrast. Too great a difference between the light side and the dark side. It's best, if you're unadventurous, to view Rhaeadr y Cwm, if you must, from a recess provided for this purpose in the dry-stone wall that borders the road that goes over the moors to the Arennigs and Bala (near where Gronw Bebyr lives). The viewpoint is two miles outwith Llan Ffestiniog.

The Afon Cynfal, after this great waterfall, performs a quick change of nature and becomes much quieter again and later, in another quite sudden transformation, it surges and swirls through a narrow and well-hidden other-world of natural oak woodland, a wood carpeted with moss and fern and whinberry bushes, lavish with river-pools and small cascades. The Afon Cynfal has entered a deep, damp, vegetated, water-worn, oak-wooded, canopied cleft and this valley is called Cwm Cynfal. The river here is fast-flowing and, after going under a stylish foot-bridge with green-painted cast-iron railings ('Bont Ddu') and past a mid-stream fern-clad pillar of rock known locally as Huw Llwyd's Pulpit ('Pulpud Huw Llwyd'), it exits, over another waterfall, the Rhaeadr Cynfal Fall, out of our story, down into Ceunant Cynfal, the next ravine, and so on, down into the Vale of Ffestiniog.

The astonishing event we are about to witness takes place near the aforesaid oak-wooded cleft in the landscape between Rhaeadr y Cwm and Rhaeadr Cynfal.

This location is of considerable drama and sensation. This is an almost unique place in Wales. It contains and sustains many very intriguing ambiguities and contrasts. Light and shade. Rushing turbulence of water and calm, cool, pools. A checker-work of oak-leaves and spangles of sunlight and sparking ripples of sun-flecked water in summer, icicles and frost and ice in winter. Gold in autumn. Green in spring. The place has a great sense and feeling of *timelessness* about it. This *is* as old as the Early Celts in Wales and yet it is, also, *now*. This is the kind of place to tell Magic (*Cyfaredd*) and Myth (*Chwedl*). If we accept that Lleu's destiny, for narrative purpose, had to happen *in reality* therefore we must also accept that it must have happened some*where* in Wales, then there can be no more suitable a place for the Welsh storyteller or the monk to have placed it than right here, between Rhaeadr y Cwm and Rhaeadr Cynfal, in Cwm Cynfal, near Llan Ffestiniog, at the head of the Vale of Ffestiniog. There is nowhere else in Wales quite like it. With the woman one loves and with the friend of one's heart, and a good library of books, one might pass an age in the Vale of Cwm Cynfal and think it but a day. Yeah.

The story specifically locates Gronw Bebyr hiding in the lee of a hill which is called Bryn Cyfergyr. This is a prominent local outcrop of rock, a remarkable and striking feature, a knuckle-like rock outcrop on a hillock, a hill, a crag, a grassy knoll to assist in the assault, known now as Bryn Cyfergyd. Bryn Cyfergyd is also the name of the Welsh farm underneath it. The hill has good vantage over the valley. A farmhouse on the opposite side of Cwm Cynfal, above Bont Newydd, is called Bryn Saeth, and this name has resonance with the 'spear' made by Gronw. His javelin, in flight, is as good a dart as any arrow. Arrow in Welsh is *saeth*. The small tributary running into the River Cynfal here at Bont Newydd is a runnel from the moors called Afon Bryn Saeth and it is *precisely* here, at its bank, on this bank of the Cynfael River, that Lleu has been lured to have his last bath. Everything fits. The geographical details today are exactly the same as they were written down over a millennium ago in Blodeuedd's instructions in her letter to Gronw.

Gronw looks out south-west from his hiding-place under cover of the crag at Bryn Cyfergyr and sees the comical condition of spreadeagle-legged Lleu. Gronw estimates the aim and steadies himself by placing one knee on the ground, half-standing up and half-sitting down. He throws the spear-javelin and it smites Lleu in the abdomen so that the shaft started out of him and the head stayed embedded. At the first moment of discovery that the arrow did strike, Lleu immediately then transforms into an eagle and the eagle rises powerfully with deep wing-beats and soars majestically up into the sky and as this eagle that is Lleu ascends it lets out of its beak a hideously eldritch, a single long echoing scream:

Aaaaaaaaaaaaaaaaaaaaaaaaaaaaaaaaaaaaaaaaaaaaaaaaaaaaaaaaaaaaaargchk!

And after that no more was seen of unfortunate Lleu Llaw Gyffes. A snowflake fell. Snow became general all over Wales. Winter had come.

(Camera *that* lot, mister Ess Pedwar Eck film-makers.)

Lleu had ripped a hole in our world and escaped immediate death by doing a remarkable double-quick metamorphosis into a Golden Eagle (*Aquila chrysaetos*) which then flew up into the sky and in so doing this Lleu left behind him an everlasting and an inscrutable mystery and this is one of the

29

Three Great Mysteries of Wales. How the fucking hell did Lleu Llaw Gyffes, Lleu the *Twp*, how did Lleu the Daft do *that*? I don't know. Gwydion, I guess, must have taught him the trick.

The eagle disappeared. The eagle vanished. Where Lleu Llaw Gyffes went to nobodaddy knows.

Blodeuedd and Gronw went blatantly back to Mur Castell straddled on a saddle on the same horse clippety-clop clippety-clop and that afternoon they slept shamelessly together as lovers and eleven (11!) engagements they had of each other (absence, they say, makes the cock grow stronger) and they were hard at it again and again for many another day and night, day and night. What a sexual apparatus! Blodeuedd howled out loud at Llys Mur Castell foul-mouthed imprecations:

– *Asterisks* me hard in my hot, wet *asterisks*! *Asterisks*! *Asterisks*! O, she giggled, pardon my queeves!

Some say Blodeuedd was sexually insatiable. Gronw Bebyr claimed lordship over Merioneth I mean Meirionnydd I mean Eifionydd and Ardudwy as well as Penllyn and the land thereafter was under his strix I mean strict I mean stringent control. Some say he looked tired.

The news travelled quickly to Castell Caernarfon and Gwydion was shocked unutterably to learn of the betrayal and the loss of Lleu like that. Gwydion, after all, had given all the love and affection he'd ever had to that lad Lleu. And that eagle-trick, he'd taught the boy, *that* was strictly for EMERGENCY USE ONLY. The transformation could not easily be undone. Only Gwydion had the key. Gwydion, in a terrible state of distress and upset and with the look of sleeplessness already upon his eyes, urgently asks compassionate leave of Math and his last words to the King before leaving were these:

– Rest I'll not have until the day I find my son.

'*My*' son. That's what Gwydion said. He'd said it at last. He had admitted it. Math understood. Math let him go.

A Father in Search of A Son

Gwydion sets out and searches Arfon and Môn and Talebolion and Eryri and Dwyfor and Eifionydd and Ardudwy and even down to the end of the Llŷn and the whole of elsewhere in Gwynedd and Powys and Clwyd but for all this travelling and scanning the sky-line with his telescope it is in vain, for any news of the eagle that is Lleu there is altogether none. Poor Gwydion. A year has passed. The task, it seems, was a hopeless undertaking. Gwydion returns. He is haggard. He is utterly dejected. His grief has had no relief. He is exhausted. He rests for the night in the estate of Maenawr Bennardd in a smallholding belonging to a tenant-farmer. And the name of that farm was Tyddyn Hwch.

By chance Gwydion happens to overhear a conversation over supper between the master of Tyddyn Hwch and his swineherd concerning the quick movements of a particular sow each morning and speculation between them as to her wandering and whereabouts it is she goes by day. Gwydion enquires on the manner of the journey that the sow does make. He is always alert to mysteries like this. The swineherd relates it to him thus:

– Every day, when the pig-sty is opened, out she goes at full trot like a shot. No one can track her she goes so quick. Neither is it known which place is her destination other than it is as if she had disappeared into Annwn or entered the London Underground. But she doth come back each night and I do put her into the pig-pen. It's a bleedin' mystery, Sir.

Ah, ah. Gwydion senses that at last he's on to something, a sign at least, a little something, that will lead him on to Lleu. So Gwydion, next morning, at day-break, by arrangement with the swineherd, waits by the gate. Out she bolts! Gwydion follows the fleet-foot *mochyn* as soon as she's released from the overnight pen. Off she trots this hefty *hwch*, upstream, up the Afon Llyfni, past two lakes and into a valley. There is a great outcrop of rock at the far end of this valley and the sow hastens straightway toward this crag. She runs up a steep cleft in that crag non-stop and there, at the top, she stops. She halts under an oak. A solitary, stunted, single old oak which is lichened and gnarled by wind and age, twisted as if in Wistman's Wood and like unto that at Gallt y Bwlch, observes Gwydion. The sow rummages at the base of this tree and there she doth feed, at its roots, most ravenously. Her snout detects with glee and with greed the gobs of good flesh that's got rotten with maggot that somehow is falling to the ground from out of that oak. What's this? What's this? What cycle of nitrogen or oxygen or molybdenum is *this?* thinks Gwydion. Gwydion looks up. At the top-most branch of that stunted oak is anchored, by grip of its talons, an eagle (though Gwydion at first sight misidentifies this eagle as but a thin kind of kite). The eagle occasionally did

shudder its body and flap its wing half-heartedly and maggoty flesh then did fall fluttering to the ground in flitches from its feathers and this sphacelation and putridity is the healthy nutrition that is received into the mouth of the sow that snouts about the ground down by Gwydion. And this discovery by Gwydion ended the mystery of the quick-foot sow owned by the tenant of Tyddyn Hwch in the estate of Maenawr Bennardd. There you go then. All is explained.

Gwydion has found the eagle that must be the eagle that is the eagle-Lleu. Gwydion sings an *englyn* to hint that he knows the eagle's true identity:

> *You are the shadow of the waxwing slain*
> *by the false azure in the window-pane;*
> *and yet you flew on* (or something like that).

The eagle's interested. The eagle comes down to the middle of the tree. Gwydion sings a second *englyn* and the eagle now comes down to the lowest bough. Closer, *Eryr*, come closer, *Aquila*. Gwydion sings a third *englyn* and the eagle is enticed at this to alight at the magician's lap. Gwydion, then, ever so gently, touches the head of this poor thin eagle with a magic wand (this had been hidden all the while up his sleeve) so that Lleu (yes! it *is* he! it *is* Lleu!), shedding the last of his eagle's feathers, emerges out of the emaciated eagle's body and into human likeness, in his own image, Lleu it is doth chrysalis himself back into this world! Yet he is now a most pitiful sight. He is nothing but bare rib and skin and bones and close to death and small as a hedgehog and his vest is torn and his trousers soiled with excrement on him. Gwydion had once seen this same condition on the men released from the concentration camps at Auschwitz and Belsen. The skeletal frame. The tight taut skin. The emaciation. The skull-like face. The empty concavity of his belly. And despair and desolation was the look in Lleu's eyes. He'd been through an awful lot. This was like a shell-shock. Post-traumatic stress disorder was Gwydion's diagnosis after the spear struck did this. I can only add that however painful the reader may think Lleu's experiences were as an eagle, for me this book still falls far short of articulating in full just how utterly distressing were some of his days. I simply could not find the words to express the utter desecration of Lleu's eagle experience. Lleu had touched the void. It was touch and go whether he'd live that night or not. Poor, poor Lleu.

The little bundle that was once Lleu lay huddled and cuddled all night in Gwydion's lap, in the comfort of Gwydion's arms, protected by a wing of the magician's colourful cloak, in this cleft of a crag in the valley that was thereafter named after him, to remember him, Nant Lleu. He's mine, thought Gwydion, I was the first to see him breathe in harmony with the galaxy. I brought him up. He's mine. Gwydion looked up at the Milky Way (the Milky Way, by the way, is '*Sarn Gwydion*' in Welsh). Lleu, just at that moment, opened his little eyes. And then a shooting star above Snowdon shot! What? What's that? What exceptional celestial sign in the sky was by both simultaneously observed at about 4 am? Why, a bright shooting star (a *seren*) above Yr Wyddfa shot!

A star precipitated in interstellar space with great apparent velocity across the firmament from Virgo (the Virgin) or was it Gemini (the Twins) where it had started and it flew above the zenith over Yr Wyddfa Fawr and beyond the star-group called the Corona Borealis and on it went toward the zodiacal sign of the Magus (the Magician) into which constellation it then in silence extinguished itself.

What's this? What's this? What mystery is this? Explain it. Interpret it. *Astrologise* it, thought Gwydion.

The Corona Borealis is a small, incomplete circlet (a silver necklace) of stars high in the northern sky situated between the constellations of Hercules and Boötes. In Welsh the *Corona Borealis* (which is Latin) is called '*Caer Arianrhod*' and in English it's known as the Northern Crown. '*Arianrhod*', here, in reference to this small stellar cluster, translates as the Silver Circle (or Crown). So; the path of the asteroid went from Virgo (or Gemini) through the Silver Ring of Arianrhod and it shot above Yr Wyddfa Fawr straight into Aries (the Ram, the Magus), right? Am I right? So? What corollary? Well then. This was reckoned, in those days, this shooting star, to be an infallible portent of the retrospective and rather surprising fact to both onlookers that *paternity* is thereby confirmed to those two standing there on Earth who simultaneously do observe it. (The same comet was last seen in a similar context on Friday June 17th 1904.) The reader had better *re*-read that comet's flight. You'll see, you'll see it all works out. It's *obvious, mun!*

Arianrhod was his (Lleu's) maternal procreatrix. Already stated. And Gwydion, by his pluck and incubation of what was at first sight only an unformed little something, a bleeding placenta (the placenta, however, is the double of the child), is thus his (Lleu's) procreator and can claim, by the nature of this act, his (Gwydion's) legal right of paternal responsibility for the child. Yes! Gwydion the Magician's his Dad! This might seem to be a bit far-fetched, I know, but the stars that night in November just said it was so.

Gwydion looked down from the stars at the little bundle in his arms. Lleu, still, still in Gwydion's arms, was born extraordinarily bend sinister, thought Gwydion, whichever way you look at it.

Preordination is the word that provides an excuse when things in one's life get beyond one's control, but this reincarnation will give Lleu Llaw Gyffes a second chance to get it right next time *if* he can survive this night, thought Gwydion.

The valley where Gwydion discovered his son is a neat west-to-east topographical gap, the Nant Lleu (Nantlle) Valley (or, as we now call it, Dyffryn Nant-Lleu, the valley where Gwydion at last found Lleu). The valley exit is guarded at the end by a distinctive rock outcrop, a crag called Clogwyn y Barcud, the Crag of the Red Kite. The Red Kite is *Milvus milvus* in Latin and in Welsh it's *Barcud*. Gwydion soon corrected this to *Aquila chrysaetos*, the Golden Eagle, though the original *mistaken* name, to Gwydion's everlasting embarrassment as a Natural Historian, was the one that was used by the Ordnance Surveyors at Math's Court, mischievously, and their 'Clogwyn y Barcud' remains as such to this day on *our* OS maps though this of course is due to an ornithological error and the name of that crag should really read 'Clogwyn yr Eryr'.

An oak stands stunted between rain and sun at the top of a gully on Clogwyn y Barcud to this day. It is a queer old oak, badly cracked and deformed, a Sessile Oak, *Quercus petraea*, and it is the second of the Three Great Oaks of Wales. *This* oak is the oak at which Lleu was once anchored. Gwydion had come upon him in the nick of time. It had taken Gwydion a year and a day. A day later and the eagle would have been dead, undoubtedly.

Gwydion that night in Nant Lleu held his little Lleu tight. Twenty-five Welsh miles away, at Llys Mur Castell, Blodeuedd was suddenly jerked wide-awake, out of sleep, screaming. She felt, very suddenly, *very* afraid. In her dream, Gwydion was charging towards her and was preparing to transform her. Gwydion, she tremulously told Gronw, Gwydion must have found her missing husband! Gronw, frightened, loudly let out a fart in the bed.

– Fuck it, he said.

Cut to next morning. Bright new day. Gwydion with great tenderness carries the pathetically small and emaciated body of what is left of Lleu back to Math's Court at Caernarfon and summoned all the best Physicians in

Gwynedd to assist in Lleu's recovery from this malignancy to gain good health and fitness again. It actually takes nine months of medical advice and the prescription and administration of herbal medicines as recommended by the Doctors (*meddygon*) at Myddfai and antibiotics and physiotherapy at Ysbyty Gwynedd at Penrhosgarnedd in Bangor before Lleu is pronounced well enough to go back to Dinas Din-Lleu with Gwydion (his dad) once again. He got better, it's true, physically at least, but he persists from here on in wearing a black cloak completely wrapped about him; and a black balaclava; strands of his yellow hair stick out like a beak; he wears a pair of

yellow-rimmed spectacles ('eye-rings'); and all the children at Math's Court laugh at him and call him '*Yr Aderyn Du*'. Lleu, you see, dressed like this, does little else but whistle that blackbird's song of his and hop about the garden all day in search it's said of *earthworms* to eat! *Ach y fi*! Poor Lleu. That ordeal as an eagle had badly unbalanced him.

He'd lost it. There was no getting away from it. Lleu had lost it.

Lleu's betrayal and mental disintegration like this must not be allowed to go unpunished was the quite sensible thinking in those days before the intervention of social workers and care-in-the-community psychiatry and leniency for criminals in the law-courts and Gwydion takes counsel of Math:

– It is time, is it not, for our company to get redress out of that, that *Cuculus canorus* that comes out of Penllyn.

– It is time, said Math.

Vengeance Comes, Vengeance Comes

Math orders the muster of the best men-at-arms stationed in army training camps in a ring around Eryri to come to assembly at a site above the River Seiont on the outskirts of Caernarfon that was later to be called by the Romans Seiontium (Segontium). This selected Special Armed Services' warband sets out for Ardudwy, going southward on Sarn Helen, heading direct as it does for Llys Mur Castell. Gwydion, on horseback, agitated, is at the forefront of that battalion.

Blodeuedd has heard a rumour of retribution in the wind and soon comes the sound of its coming on the ground. She quickly packs her personal things into a locked box, a cabin trunk containing her calico dresses and best cotton underclothes and other silk secrets and gossamer things, for she and her sapphic sisters intend to take the risk of trying to escape to a place prepared for that purpose up in the Manod mountains. '*Manod*' is an Old Welsh word for fine, drifting snow of the dangerous kind that blows about in the wind in such high places. Blodeuedd is insistent:

– Quick! Ke-wick! Flee! Flee! Flee with me!

Blodeuedd and the girls hurriedly depart out of the grounds of Mur Castell and over Cynfael River they hastened going upward toward a place of concealment and this place was known to them as Bryn y Castell. They retreat over what is difficult terrain at the best of times, all quags and mires and quaking bog, and all look backwards all the while in fear and fright, as well they might. And the maidens, running on ahead, pissing themselves with fright, fell into a lake and all were drowned save Blodeuedd alone. An autumnal mist had settled itself on the moor and no feature was there to guide them. A warning *had* been issued earlier that day by Cardiff Weather Centre but they, like many other foolhardy and ill-clad walkers out in the mountains of Eryri today, had, they had, simply, ignored it. All the girls were drowned. The bodies of the maidens in their summer frocks alone floated about bloated on the surface of the lake, decomposing slowly into rot and stink and skull. And that is why this pleasant lake today is called Llyn Morwynion, the Lake of the Maidens. (Not many fishermen on the bank of Llyn Morwynion know this.) Blodeuedd hesitates at the edge of this elemental end. Will she? Won't she? Should she? Why shouldn't she? Why *didn't* she?

Llyn Morwynion is a large but actually quite shallow lake at the peaty edge of the moors of Y Migneint two miles east of the village of Llan Ffestiniog. Many attribute the meaning of the name Llan Ffestiniog to the Latin *festino* which means 'to hurry', referring, they say, to the fact that Blodeuedd and her handmaidens did not linger there but hurried quickly past this place in their impetuous flight to get quick to Bryn y Castell. They made it only to the lake. Llyn Morwynion at this lofty lip overlooks close at hand the Upper Cynfal Valley, and it's from this direction that Gwydion is thunderously coming in great anger he has intending to inflict his vengeance and revenge on Blodeuedd. *And* her frigging handmaidens. Handmaidens, eh.

To come up and stumble over that edge of the valley and onto the moorland above *backward* would be quite a demanding undertaking in itself but then to proceed to fall into the lake and drown would require a very unusual degree of carelessness even for an inexperienced party of schoolgirls today. The young handmaidens were obviously unaccustomed to moorland navigation. It *is* true that certain isolated geographical locations in Eryri *do* have a nasty habit of attracting fatal accidents, but *this* shallow lake certainly is not one of them. This drowning sequence is altogether a rather awkward episode in the story and it seems to have been included in *The Mabinogion* only for the purpose of explaining the name that the lake had already by then acquired. This lake had a name-tag all ready. Llyn Morwynion is the name of this lake. Unsuspecting women walkers are sometimes known to stumble into it even to this day.

Blodeuedd and her handmaidens were heading for Bryn y Castell, a safe retreat, a hide-out, a *caer-bach*. Bryn y Castell is a flat-topped sharp-fronted hill-fort with an impeccable archaeological claim to belong to the Iron Age.

It is an attenuated hill (*bryn*) ringed by a stone wall on top, with stone huts in the flat interior, a good fortification (a *castell*), a safe house for Blodeuedd and her handmaidens to retreat. But they did not make it to Bryn y Castell. I really can't understand why Blodeuedd in fleeing away didn't stay on the path clearly marked '*Sarn Helen*' on the map, that takes one from Mur Castell safely across the high moors to Nant Conwy and the Roman Camp at Canovium and this runs right *past* Bryn y Castell. Mistakes like this, though, are still made even to this day. Snowdonia is a perilous playground.

A mile to the west of Llyn Morwynion, near Bryn y Castell, it's a bleak and desolate place and here on the moor amongst the tall thistles is a cluster of five, old, burial-stones. They are known to us in the know as '*Beddau Morynion (sic) Ardudwy*', the Graves of the Maidens of Ardudwy. The graves today are indicated only by a number of grassed-over mounds and collapsed stones half-buried in the rough turf and lichened with age, and they are not easy to find. They are marked on the map as '*Pillow Mounds*' (in Cloister Black Normal characters) on the way up to Bryn y Castell. This is all that now remains to mark the graves of Catrin and Caitlin and Jacqui and Elen and Iseullt, the handmaidens (handmaidens, eh) who were drowned not far away in the lake that now sadly commemorates them, Llyn Morwynion. Why *did* Blodeuedd hesitate? She must have known that something *bad* was about to happen.

Gwydion comes. Blodeuedd knows that something truly terrifying, something nasty, something agonising, something transforming, is about to happen to her anatomy. She'd dreamed it, had woken up screaming from the nightmare of it, four pages ago. An anguished voice inside her head is crying it out:

– Don't *do* this to me, Father. Don't *do* this to me, Dad. You never, you never allowed me to be a *child*, Dad. Oh; *please* don't *do* this to me, Dad.

Gwydion comes. Gwydion comes galloping up on his great shire-horse thntherathn thntherathn and catches up with Blodeuedd. She stands there trembling in her shift alone at the edge of Llyn Morwynion. Gwydion is beside himself with rage and wrath and at first he can't jay anything at her but screech at her and these are the sounds that he made:

Skaaaaaaaaak! Skaaaaaaaaaak! Skaaaaaaaaaaaaak!

Thereafter, composing himself, Gwydion speaks a speech to Lleu Llaw Gyffes' wife that had become so indiscreetly unfaithful to Lleu, and his murderess too, and this is Gwydion's speech to Blodeuedd (it is in fact the longest monologue in the whole of *The Mabinogion*):

– I will. I will. I will not kill thee outright. I will do much worse than slaughter to thee, that which King Math and I made sweet and honest and so beautiful as Flower-Maiden. And it is this, you fucking little bitch. I will let thee go. I will let thee go. In the form of a bird. A bird, Blodeuedd. And because of the dishonour and disgrace and anguish that thou hast done to thy husband and to this court, thou art never to dare to show thy pretty little false face in the light of day ever again. Because. Because you will be afraid of all other birds, Blodeuedd. There will be enmity everlasting between thee and all other birds, Blodeuedd. It will be their nature to mob and molest and pester and screech loudly at thee wherever they may find thee by day. And you will be known as... as... what's your fucking name, you fucking cunt, you... you... you *counterfeit*, that's it, that's it, I've got it now, I curse thee with it, I name thee with it, I name thee **Blodeuwedd**.

And straightway at the end of this curse Gwydion struck Blodeuedd and magicked her into an owl. An owl! Don't ask me how he did it.

And that is how the owl received its name in our language (*Y Gymraeg*). Blodeuwedd means 'Flower-Face' in Welsh. This is no bad name for the name of the owl.

The Tawny Owl, *Strix aluco*, is streaked with tawny-coloured stripes and so it is indeed in Cymraeg, *Tylluan Frech*, the Brinded Owl. This owl is a rich chestnut in general colour, buff, tawny, brown, mottled buff, *melynddu* in Welsh, broadly streaked in browns like this on wing and face and back and breast. The facial disc is set unusually with two large forward-facing black eyes. The Tawny Owl is seldom seen by day. It is, strictly, a nocturnal owl. The voice or sound that it makes is a long drawn-out tri-syllabic quavering hoot, a hooted '*hoo-hoo-hoo-oo-oo-ooo*', and also there occur sharp, harsh, '*ke-wick, ke-wick*'s. These notes are the origin of the traditional anthropovocalised '*tu-whit, tu-whoo*'s in children's literature. Owlets – juvenile owls – emit sounds remarkably like the opening grate of a rusty back-garden gate or a heavy oak door which creaks when it did open.

The Tawny Owl inhabits deciduous woodlands and nests in a hole in a tree. It feeds on small mammals and birds, hunting its prey at night. The Owl sits still on a branch close to the main trunk of a tree in daytime, attempting to sleep, impassively, eyes half-shut, to get some sleep, but she is constantly bothered and is very often mobbed by the retributive attacks of many a woodland bird and she (Blodeuwedd) is scolded at most loudly by the Blackbird (*Turdus merula*) (*Mwyalchen* in Welsh) (the cock is distinctive) and that brightly-coloured corvid the Jay (*Garrulus glandarius*). The Jay's harsh scolding scream goes something like '*skaaak, skaaak*' and in Welsh this crow is called *Ysgrech y Coed*, the 'Screech of the Wood'.

Gwydion used to begin his famous series of illustrated lectures on Welsh History, *Hanes Cymru*, hilariously, thus:

– The Jay has a great liking for acorns. The Jay collects them in autumn and can carry several acorns in its beak at a time. The Jay takes these acorns from out of existing woods and buries them in surrounding fields out in the open. I'll eat some of these acorns later, says the

Jay; but then forgets where most of the scattered acorns are kept! The acorns start to germinate, and grow. An oak will grow out of each of these. Jays, in this manner, may well have helped the great forests of Oak to spread westward across the continent of Europe immediately after the last of the great Ice Ages retreated. And this also is the way in which the Welsh got to Wales.

Gwydion then abruptly bursts into the audience flicking his blue-and-white cloak about with its hood erected screeching '*Skaaak! Skaaak! Skaaak!*' at his astonished students, in Welsh! Gwydion the Magician, they said, is the best narrator of Natural History tales in Wales!

The Blackbird and the Jay are the reincarnations today of Lleu and Gwydion (of course! of course!) though present-day theologists and ornithologists do *scoff* at the thought of this and that Blodeuedd was turned into a Tawny Owl. But a belief in the transmigration of our souls like this, across the ages, across natural barriers, reincarnation into animals and undines and nymphs, for example, transmogrification like this, metempsychosis they used to call it, was once an idea universally held amongst the Welsh and Irish Celts and there are still those among us in Wales and in Ireland today with a similar sensitivity and respect for the little creatures of our woodlands and lakes and waterfalls and and Nature, and *we* do not so lightly dismiss this possibility of continuity like do so many others elsewhere out there in the in the Christian world today. It is certainly true that what you might hear is *Blodeuwedd*'s voice in that oak outside your house at night and she is bemoaning the fact of her eternal damnation at the hand of Gwydion. This is not superstition. This is not Celtic Romance. I'm not pulling your leg. This is *Science* and Ornithology. Ask the RSPB. Listen. Listen. *Tu-whit, tu-whoo. Tu-whit, tu-whooo.* That's not the sound of any old owl. *That*'s the hoot of Blodeuwedd.

(In Wales, the hooting of an owl not only signifies the loss of a maiden's virginity but also it presages, it presages a death.)

Gronw Bebyr had earlier made his cowardly escape across the moorlands and hills and the Lliw Valley to his manor-house at Caer Gai, Plas Quilty

('*Quilty*' is an English corruption of the Welsh *Gwyllt-tŷ*, the Wild House, the Mad-House, the Perverse Place), at Llanuwchllyn, at the end of Llyn Tegid at Bala, at the end of an arm of the Arans, and from this corrupt court came message after message from Gronw to Lleu offering land in Wales or territories in Lloegr or gold or silver or a hundred Welsh Blacks or sheep or pigs or his geese or his wife or his eleven year-old daughter Dolores or any young untouched monastic student (male or female) that would do *anything* for him or any young thing or anyone else in compensation for the cuckoldry and that nasty injury that he (Gronw) had unintentionally inflicted by accident, by mistake, it was all a mistake, a stupid mistake, could not he be forgiven, you see it was just because of one *silly* act in summer (one spontaneous physical engagement he'd had, is all) and all consequent was a misunderstanding. Let's be *friends*, Lleu. P.S., I will, if you want it that way, if it pleases you to have it that way, I will act it that way, as thy mate. Lleu answered:

– I will not accept any of this. The redress that I demand is that he position himself as target at the same such place where once I was when he aimed that ill-got arrow at me. And I then will position myself at that same place where once *he* hid and I will then launch a spear at *him*. This is the single and only reparation that I, Lord Gyffes, demand of he that is guilty. Tell the... tell the *cuckoo* that.

Gronw recognises exactly what kind of eternity is being so obligingly and so inexorably spread out before him and he accepts the fact, at last, that he has no defence to go against it. Unless! Unless he can substitute someone else! He asks, each in turn, his brothers, his gentlemen, his administrators, his clerks, his gardener, his lackeys, even the rank and file of his soldiers who are all poxed, to take themselves to that appointed place to place themselves there in his stead.

– Sorry, *Sais*, came the unanimous reply from each and every man he asked.

The whole company at Parc Quilty *refused*! There's *disloyalty* for you, thought Gronw. The Welsh are a disloyal lot even to this day.

43

Typical Welsh. Never *trust* a Welshman. Thieves and schemers and layabouts and lunatics and self-styled poets and madmen the whole fuckin' lot of them. The Welsh are an *odd* lot, thought Gronw. (Gronw, it turned out, was from Lloegr (England) or Ffrainc (France) or even from as far away as Yr Almaen (Germany). Whichever, Gronw was one of the very first Saxons (*Sais*) to come into Cymru (Wales). The first in-migrant, you might say. And 'Gronw Bebyr' was an *alias*! His real name was 'Groaner' Bukker. He *was* strong. He *was* a buck. He *was* vigorous. He *was* enthusiastic. Also, alas, as we've observed, 'Groaner' was also a, a *wanker*. Masturbated. He got himself off dressed up in the cathexis of women's used underclothes. *Ach y fi! Ach y fi!* No *Welsh*man would do that.)

Gronw Bebyr was dragged in disgrace back to the bank of the Cynfael River. He was placed in position at exactly the same place where Lleu had had his bath, beside the brook called Afon Bryn Saeth. How prettily did sound the run of that water to the man that is about to die! A Jay is out collecting acorns to bury, garrulously, in and out of the canopy of Cynfael Wood (Coed Cynfal) (it is, of course, by now, again, November). Lleu gets into position at the knoll that is known as Bryn Cyfergyr. Gronw sinks down on his bended knees, in a boggy bit, and begs Lord Lleu to *please* re-think this reverse arrangement:

– Honest, Lleu, it really wasn't *my* fault. It was she, thy incontinent wife, it was *she* that did seduce *me*. I was innocent of that first offence and not the other way round as usually it doth happen. I gave her a cormorant (*Phalacrocorax carbo*) for her birthday. She said she'd rather have a shag (*Phalacrocorax aristotelis*). And later. Well. Well, I can explain that. Women's tricks and stratagems and arts and use of underwear it was made me do to thee that which I was *instructed* to do to thee from the position where now thou dost stand and seeth me and taketh aim at me and oh, Lord Gyffes, WAIT! I am naked and defenceless and consequently, Your Highness, cans't thou not let me have just a little something, an iron shield maybe, a tree, an oak tree, a stone, *this* stone, this slab that here I see at this brook-bank how sweetly doth this river sound to me, this flat stone slab that convenient Fate now doth offer this as shield to me, so that I may stand this slab, if you'll just allow me, to lift, it up, like this, like so, to place it as a protection between you and me against the *very* severe blow which thou, I know, will throw. Your Holiness! Pity me. Grant me this at least. – I will not refuse thee that, said our Hero.

Gronw, it seems, was completely unaware of the legendary story of how Lord Gyffes got his name. What difference would it make whether or not Gronw had this puny piece of stone protection against an arrow or bolt thrown by the Fair-Hand-Deft even though it be thrown from so afar away as Bryn Cyfergyr. None whatsofuckingever.

Gronw stands with the slightly tapering slab set upright in front of him, shivering with fright, as well he might, on a bank of the Afon Bryn Saeth. All is hush. All is expectant. The brook alone babbles and cascades in a watercourse above and a Blackbird somewhere in the distance sings, over by Bryn Cyfergyr. Lleu Llaw Gyffes takes aim with the best weapon of war given to him by his mother Arianrhod. The strength that enters his arm is granted to him by the training and the wisdom of his father Gwydion. Lleu draws back the spear and with all his strength and calculation and a grunt of catharsis that he *never* had with Blodeuedd, he lets his arrow fly. Time seems to slow down at moments like this. Survivors of motorcar accidents report the same time dilatation. The arrow hurtles. Interesting it would be to investigate the aerodynamics and aerial Physics of its flight. The arrow rushes through air, though now it seems as though suspended, over valley and the rooftop and the chimney-pots of Bryn Saeth farm. The arrow comes onward and closer and closer to seek out the place whereat it was aimed. The arrow is aimed to strike its target right at the very heart and the aim of Lleu Llaw Gyffes has been dead right. The spear strikes, straight, through stone, flesh, blood and bone and back-bone, and only an Oak in the background could halt it. A Jay, startled, comes out of the Oak. Acorns are scattered all over Cwm Cynfael by the impact.

And this tells how Gronw Bebyr was slain stone-dead by the javelin of Lleu Llaw Gyffes.

Believe it or believe it not, this *is* a true story that I tell. Well; the audience willingly suspended their disbelief in *those* days, long ago now, when first I told it. They believed it! Every word of it! Every word that was spoken. But *now*adays. I begin to detect by the unrest increasingly evident among the audience tonight that some of you, the more sophisticated shall we say, the more 'cultured', who read this, do not believe a word of this, do you. I can, quite easily, identify you: historians and intellectuals, agnostic and academic, sceptic and rationalist, horny theologist and scientist, eh? Well, I tell you, all, it's the truth not only of myth that I tell. Come and take a look at *this*. There! There it is! None of yous can contradict *that*! Here the stone is, look, on a bank of the Cynfal River, facing Bryn Cyfergyd, with the hole of the spear straight through it and true. This is Llech Ronw. This is the Slab of Gronw.

Llech Ronw lies neglected and moss-covered at a rather unsightly site on the right bank of the Afon Bryn Saeth, a small tributary running into the Afon Cynfal, within sight of the farm-house of Bryn Saeth, at Bont Newydd, near Llan Ffestiniog in Ardudwy. Llech Ronw is a flat, slightly tapering, rectangular stone slab 5′ 6″ in height from toe to top whatever that is in modern metric measurement with a circular hole about 4½″ in diameter approximately 5″ from the top (the 'head') end. If a 6ft man like Gronw Bebyr were to stand behind it, then the hole situates itself slightly on the left side of the man's thorax immediately in front of the heart. This is it. It fits perfectly. It faces Bryn Cyfergyr. The measurements are exactly the same as in *The Mabinogion*.

The distance from Bryn Cyfergyr to Llech Ronw by line of sight and by direct arrow-flight is a distance of well over half a mile. The strength and accuracy of Lleu Llaw Gyffes' adept throw (his deft spear-shot), though great the gap, is not at all in doubt. The Fair One hit the slab with a very deft-hand delivery indeed. It was a dab shot! The name of the man wasn't so daft after all, as Gwydion had first thought it. Arianrhod was right. She'd foreseen that all this was going to happen to her son (his conception, his youthful exploits in the company of Gwydion, his exile by transformation into a kite, his psychosis, his recuperation, his rehabilitation, this deft spear-shot). She had laboured by three curses placed upon her son to prevent the trauma of it all happening to him, but Arianrhod *couldn't* stop the working out of its prophecy and predestination. At last Lleu's destiny is now all but done. That's it. It's over. Gronw Bebyr was slain by the spear of Lleu Llaw Gyffes.

And there that stone still is, reader, on a bank of the Cynfael River, with a hole of the shaft of the arrow pierced through it straight and true. Prove it. Quest it. Inspect it. The stone with the hole in it. See, pilgrim. It all works out. This *is* the Slab of Gronw! In a world in which so much is fake it shocks you to come up against something so, so real. This is serious. This is no toy. This *is* the real thing. This is not a gate-post. This stone is straight out of *The Mabinogion*. This is a true story that I did tell.

The National Museum of Wales or the Welsh Assembly really *ought* to go there to collect and protect (*cadw*) it because this nationally famous stone, this historic monument, Llech Ronw, is liable otherwise to get broken or vandalised where it now lies and it could get stolen and end up in somebody's back garden or else in a private collection or the farmer at Bryn Saeth farm might embed it, upright, in concrete, with the hole facing in the wrong fucking direction and that would be a great loss not only to Gwynedd but also to the Welsh literary establishment and great libraries of Wales.

An Oak grows solidly behind Llech Ronw and Broom is in profusion in June. The milky heads of Meadowsweet grow thickly close by it, and the flowers of it stink of goat. Llech Ronw lies neglected like this, on a bank of the babbling Afon Bryn Saeth.

Hic jacet Gronw Bebyr.

The End

Lleu Llaw Gyffes accepts back his lost landlordship over all the lands of Eifionydd and Ardudwy and for the second time in the story of his life Lord Gyffes ruled kindly over this *cantref* that was his kingdom and it did thereafter prosper. And, as the tale tells it, in time, and with the blessing of Gwydion and Math, Lord Gyffes became King of Gwynedd in the end. (And that's exactly when the trouble with Cantref Gwaelod started! But *that's* another story.)

And this ends The Fourth Branch of *The Mabinogi*.

WAIT! Wait a moment, please. Please remain seated, ladies and gentlemen, for I have the ability to conjure up a more, a more creative conclusion to this evening's entertainment than you'd expect from *that*, that rather abrupt ending in *The Mabinogion*. All hush, please. All be expectant. Listen. Listen to this. Then you can go.

And so. So if today you should come to wander into this part of the land of Britain that is known to us as Cymru and you happen in passing to see oak or eagle, blackbird, jay, cuckoo, reef of rock or seal or owl, know thee then that in this place these living creatures today are but the *re*-created creatures of the actors and actresses once known in our Welsh Myths as Math ap Mathonwy and Lleu Llaw Gyffes and Gwydion the Magician and Gronw Bebyr and Arianrhod and Dylan the Sea-Creature and Blodeuwedd the Owl. Treat kindly these places and this people of Wales and this flora and fauna of our vulnerable Welsh countryside. Do them no harm. Do them no insult. Do them no injury. Because. Because if you do. Because if you do, the casualty, next time, like me, could be you. *Nos da.*

Y DIWEDD

Also Published by

Aberdyfi: The Past Recalled – Hugh M. Lewis £6.95
You Don't Speak Welsh! – Sandi Thomas £5.95
Ar Bwys y Ffald – Gwilym Jenkins £7.95
Come, Wake the Dragon – Rodney Aitchtey £5.95

For more information about the Dinas imprint
contact Lefi Gruffudd at

y Lolfa

Y Lolfa Cyf., Talybont, Ceredigion SY24 5AP
e-mail ylolfa@ylolfa.com
website www.ylolfa.com
tel. (01970) 832 304
fax 832 782
isdn 832 813